Daniel Finds a Poem

Micha Archer

Nancy Paulsen Books

For Danny and Edgar

NANCY PAULSEN BOOKS

an imprint of Penguin Random House LLC
375 Hudson Street, New York, NY 10014

Library of Congress Cataloging-in-Publication Data
Archer, Micha, author, illustrator.
Daniel finds a poem / Micha Archer.
pages cm
Summary: A little boy's animal friends help him discover
the poetry to be found in nature.
[1. Poetry—Fiction. 2. Nature—Fiction. 3. Animals—Fiction.] I. Title.
PZ7.A67475Dan 2016
[Fic]—dc23
2015009190

Manufactured in China by RR Donnelley Asia Printing Solutions Ltd.
ISBN 978-0-399-16913-7
Special Markets ISBN 978-1-524-73961-4
10 9 8 7 6 5 4 3 2 1

Design by Ryan Thomann. Text set in Paper Cuts.
The illustrations were done in oil and collage,
using tissue paper and patterned papers
created with homemade stamps.

Daniel knows all the rocks, trees, and animals in the park.

On Monday morning,
Daniel sees something new
on the park gate. A sign reads,
POETRY IN THE PARK
SUNDAY AT 6 O'CLOCK

"What is
poetry?"
Daniel says.

POETRY
in the
PARK
SUNDAY
AT
6 o'clock

He looks up in surprise
when he hears Spider say,

"To me, poetry is when morning dew glistens."

On Tuesday, Daniel climbs the old oak tree. He sees Squirrel. "Squirrel, do you know what poetry is?"

"Poetry is when
crisp leaves crunch,"
Squirrel tells him.

On Wednesday,
Daniel calls into Chipmunk's hole,
"Chipmunk, can you tell me
what poetry is?"

"Poetry? Hmmm. Poetry is a home with many windows in an old stone wall."

On Thursday, Daniel makes a boat with a leaf for a sail and watches the wind carry it across the pond. He calls quietly to Frog, "Excuse me, Frog. What is poetry?"

"Poetry," says Frog,
"is a cool pool to dive into."

On Friday, Daniel parts the cattails and finds Turtle. "Hello, Turtle. I have a question. Do you know what poetry is?"

"I think poetry
is sun-warmed
sand," Turtle says.

On Saturday afternoon,
Daniel finds Cricket
in the shade of the slide.

When the shadows
are long, Cricket fills
the air with music.

"Is this poetry
to you, Cricket?"

"Singing at twilight
when the day is done?
Indeed it is, Daniel."

That night, moonlight fills Daniel's room.
He hears a *who*. Leaning from his window,
he calls to Owl, "Owl, what is poetry?"

"Oh, poetry! Poetry is bright stars
in the branches, moonlight on the grass,
and silent wings to take me wherever I go.
Good night, dear Daniel," she whispers,
and flies off into the night.

On Sunday, the sun wakes up Daniel.
He is happy when he remembers it's Sunday.

"Today is Poetry in the Park," says Daniel,
"and I have a poem!"

Morning dew glistens,
Crisp leaves crunch,
There's a home with many windows
in the old stone wall.
Cool pools to dive in,
Sun-warmed sand to lie in,
Singing at twilight when
the day is done.
Bright stars in the branches,
Moonlight on the grass,
And silent wings to take me
wherever I go.

On the way home, Daniel stops to watch the sunset sky reflecting in the pond.

"That looks like poetry to me."

"To me too," says Dragonfly.